Stitched in Love

Penelope Rosewood

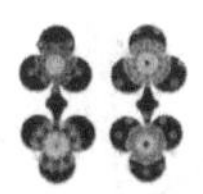

Four of Clubs Publishing

Print ISBN: 978-1-7636295-1-6

E-book ISBN: 978-1-7636295-0-9

Published by Four of Clubs, Sydney, Australia.

Email: info.fourclubs@gmail.com

Chapter 1

Stitches

In the bustling emergency room of St. Gabriel's Hospital, the air was thick with a sense of urgency and the scent of antiseptic. Amidst the flurry of doctors, nurses, and patients, an attending physician named Mia stood with unwavering focus. Her sharp eyes scanned the room, absorbing every detail and calculating the next move. Dressed in her crisp white coat, Mia exuded an air of professionalism and determination, her every action guided by cold logic. At thirty-something years old, Mia had already gained valuable experience and was highly regarded for her skills in the fast-paced environment of the ER.

On this particular evening, fate had something unexpected in store for Mia. Just as she was about to review a patient's chart, the swinging doors burst open, and in walked a firefighter. Her presence was like a burst of energy, drawing all eyes towards her. Strong and confident, she exuded a commanding presence. Her strong facial features and curly hair, tied up in a bun, added to her aura of resilience and determination.

Clutching her arm, the firefighter winced slightly, the deep cut on her forearm staining her uniform with crimson. The room hushed momentarily, captivated by her entrance. With a warm smile, she approached the triage desk, her energy contagious, and her voice carrying a melodic timbre.

"Hey there," she greeted the receptionist with a warm smile. "I had a little mishap at work. Could you help me get patched up?"

Mia, hearing the exchange, couldn't help but be intrigued. Her curiosity drew her gaze to the firefighter's injured arm. She watched as the firefighter's smile faded, replaced by a hint of discomfort. It was a rare moment of vulnerability that flickered across her face before being masked by her usual cheerfulness.

Not one to be swayed by emotions, Mia stepped forward, her voice steady and professional. "I'll take care of it," she offered, her tone devoid of warmth, yet laced with an underlying curiosity.

Mia's eyes met with the firefighters, and for a brief moment, the two women shared a connection that transcended their disparate personalities. It was as if time slowed down, and within that infinitesimal moment, an invisible thread linked them together.

"I'm Dr. Mia Carella," Mia broke the silence, her voice clear and composed. The firefighter met her gaze and offered a warm smile. "I'm Jacqueline Rivera, but you can call me Jackie. Nice to meet you."

Mia's initial surprise morphed into a subtle nod, her features settling back into a mask of professional detachment. She maintained eye contact with Jackie, her expression unreadable for a moment before she responded in a controlled tone, "Nice to meet you too." Despite the warmth in Jackie's greeting, Mia's demeanor remained cool and businesslike. "Please follow me," she continued, gesturing towards the treatment area. Leading the way through the busy emergency room, Mia navigated with practiced efficiency towards a quieter corner reserved for immediate patient care.

"Please take a seat," Mia instructed, guiding Jackie to a nearby bed in the treatment area. Jackie complied, sitting down with a slight wince of pain as she adjusted herself. The contrast between them was undeniable. Mia, methodical and cool-headed, prepared the medical supplies, her mind already mapping out the necessary steps. Meanwhile, Jackie couldn't help but fidget, her vibrancy emanating even in the face of injury.

"So, Do you come here often?" Jackie teased, a playful grin tugging at the corners of her lips.

Mia arched an eyebrow, caught off guard by the firefighter's humor. "Only when I'm working," she replied dryly, attempting to maintain her professional composure.

Jackie chuckled, undeterred by Mia's reserved response. "Well, lucky me then," she remarked, earning a small smile from Mia, almost imperceptible to the casual observer.

With a gentle touch, Mia began examining the deep cut on Jackie's arm and the small cut on her forehead. Her hands moved with practiced precision, her medical instincts taking over. As she worked, she couldn't help but feel a sense of curiosity. "So, what happened?" she asked, her voice filled with both professional concern and a hint of genuine interest.

"We got a call about a fire in a residential building. It was an old house," Jackie explained, her tone steady. "Everything went well, and we got everyone out. I took off my jacket to give to a civilian for protection, and just as I did, a piece of timber came loose and struck my arm, catching me off guard."

"Well, that's quite a story," Mia responded, her voice a delicate balance of intrigue and concern. She examined the deep cut on Jackie's arm and the smaller cut on her forehead with a practiced eye. After a moment of thoughtful silence, Mia continued, her tone steady yet compassionate, "These wounds will need several stitches to properly heal." She reached for the necessary supplies, her mind already focused on providing the best care for Jackie's injuries.

As Mia carefully cleaned and sterilized Jackie's deep cut, her hands moved with precision and expertise. The dim light of the treatment room cast a gentle glow, illuminating their faces in its soft embrace. Mia, usually focused solely on her work, couldn't help but notice the delicate features of Jackie's face as she delicately stitched up her forehead.

Their eyes locked, Mia peering intently into Jackie's mesmerizing eyes. The usual coldness in Mia's gaze softened momentarily, a hint of warmth flickering beneath her professional facade. Her heart fluttered, a feeling she hadn't experienced in a long time.

Jackie, seemingly oblivious to the captivating effect she had on Mia, continued to pepper her with lighthearted questions, her voice a playful melody amidst the serious atmosphere.

A playful smile danced on Jackie's lips as she couldn't resist teasing her. "Let me guess, Aquarius?" she remarked, her tone filled with a hint of mischief.

Mia arched an eyebrow, a subtle hint of skepticism in her gaze. "Aquarius? What do you mean, my star sign?" Her eyes met Jackie's, momentarily surprised by the remark. "What? You don't actually think I believe in that stuff," she retorted, her voice tinged with dry skepticism.

Mia prided herself on her logical and analytical nature, dismissing anything that veered into the realm of the mystical or unscientific.

Jackie chuckled, her laughter laced with warmth. "You'd be surprised how accurate it can be," she replied, her gaze unwavering. "Logical, detached, analytical, reserved...You tick the boxes, Doc."

Mia couldn't help but raise an eyebrow, her curiosity piqued. "And what does that mean?" she asked, her voice laced with a mixture of amusement and intrigue.

Jackie leaned back, crossing her arms, and pondered for a moment. "Aquarius, the water bearer," she began. "Independent, innovative, and often known for their intellectual pursuits. They can be both logical and compassionate, but sometimes struggle with fully expressing their emotions. And from what I've seen so far, you seem to tick all the boxes."

Mia's lips curled into a faint smile, a hint of recognition in her eyes. She hadn't expected Jackie to be so perceptive, to see through the walls she had built around her heart. "You really believe in all this astrology stuff?" she asked, a touch of curiosity in her voice.

Jackie expresses, "I've seen astrology work wonders. I use it as a psychological tool to better understand people. It's like a language of symbols, and it helps me work more effectively with individuals and build stronger relationships. I consider myself an investigator of human nature."

Jackie leaned forward, her eyes filled with genuine enthusiasm. "How can you truly know a person? I mean, there are all these personality tests out there, but they only seem to scratch the surface. Astrology, on the other hand, is like a magnifying glass. It allows you to gain valuable insights into people's inner worlds— their hobbies, family, past and struggles. It's like peering into the depths of their psyche and unraveling the complexities of their personalities. That's what I like about it... I want to understand people."

Mia glanced up from her work, meeting Jackie's eyes once again. A flicker of something more than professional interest passed between them. Quickly averting her gaze, Mia refocused on her task, determined to maintain professionalism.

Jackie's words surprised her; she hadn't encountered someone genuinely interested in human behavior before. It made Mia realize how disconnected she had become since pursuing medicine. She had forgotten her own initial drive to understand and help people on a deeper level through medicine. The struggles and hardships she endured to become a physician had led her to bury her emotions, shielding herself from the emotional toll the job could take.

"Are you an Aquarius then?" Jackie interrupted Mia's thoughts.

"Yeah, that's right actually, I am an Aquarius," Mia replied.

"I knew it!" exclaimed Jackie enthusiastically.

"That's a nice party trick you've got there," said Mia with a hint of sarcasm.

"So what are you? What's your sign?" she added, genuinely curious.

Jackie smiled cheekily at Mia. "Why don't you take a guess? Come on, describe what you see," Jackie challenged.

Mia paused, then grinned. "You seem curious and philosophical. You're a firefighter, so there's an element of bravery there. I don't know what sign that is.

Jackie paused, then grinned mischievously. "I'm a Sag! Sagittarius, ta daaa," she laughed. "A fire sign, and I love running into burning buildings. I do have Mercury and Venus in Scorpio, which explains the interest in all things deep and mysterious, but I'll save that topic for next time. Don't want to overwhelm you now, do we?"

Mia stood there, a mix of confusion and amusement playing on her face as she observed the vibrant personality sitting before her. Jackie's infectious joy made Mia feel emotions she hadn't experienced in a long time. It was as if a fire had been ignited within her, though she wasn't quite sure how she felt about that.

"Aquarius and Sagittarius are highly compatible, just so you know," Jackie added casually. Mia pretended not to hear that, focusing instead on finishing the last stitch on Jackie's forehead.

"Done," Mia stated, her voice steady but with an underlying softness. "You should be fine now. Just keep it clean and avoid any further injury."

Jackie grinned, her eyes sparkling with a mixture of gratitude and something else, a glimmer of recognition, perhaps. "Thank You," she said, her voice filled with sincerity. "I owe you one."

Mia nodded, acknowledging the gratitude with a subtle nod. "It's my job," she replied, her tone less dismissive than before.

The moment lingered, their eyes locked in a silent exchange. Mia fought against the growing attraction she felt, reminding herself of the boundaries that should remain in place. But Jackie's presence, her light-hearted nature, and the way she effortlessly drew a grin from Mia's lips made it increasingly challenging to resist.

Mia then moved on to the cut on Jackie's arm, carefully examining it. "Now let's stitch this arm up," she said calmly, preparing her materials to tend to the wound with focused expertise.

Mia had just begun to gently tend to Jackie's wound when the atmosphere suddenly shifted when Jackie's walkie-talkie buzzed to life with urgency. Jackie's expression turned serious in an instant, her eyes focused and determined. She reached for the radio and responded swiftly, her voice steady and filled with authority.

"This is Lieutenant Rivera. I copy, over," she replied, her tone commanding and decisive.

Mia observed the transformation in Jackie, her vibrant demeanor fading momentarily as she took on the role of a dedicated firefighter.

Her heart skipped a beat as she witnessed the depths of Jackie's strength and bravery unfold before her eyes.

After reporting back, Jackie turned to Mia, a playful smile tugging at the corner of her lips. "Sorry, Doctor Carella. I'm gonna have to cut this short. Can you patch me up later? A little band-aid will do for now," she quipped, trying to maintain a sense of lightness amidst the seriousness of the situation.

Mia was momentarily taken aback, her hands hesitating mid-stitch. She had not expected their brief encounter to be interrupted so abruptly. Yet, her professionalism resurfaced as she swiftly gathered her composure.

"But I'm not done yet," Mia protested, her voice betraying a trace of disappointment.

"Don't worry, you'll get to finish your work of art once I get back," Jackie reassured Mia with a playful grin before heading off.

Mia couldn't help but feel a mixture of excitement and trepidation at Jackie's words. The unexpected connection between them had ignited a longing within her, one she hadn't anticipated. She watched as Jackie turned to leave, her vibrant presence slowly retreating from the room.

As Jackie reached the door, she glanced back at Mia with warmth, leaving her with a reassuring smile before disappearing into the corridor. Mia couldn't help but feel a rush of emotions, a mixture of curiosity, attraction, and the slightest hint of longing. She watched as Jackie disappeared through the door, leaving behind a void that seemed to echo with the promise of something more.

With a deep breath, Mia returned to her workstation, her mind filled with thoughts of Jackie. The encounter had sparked a fire within her, awakening emotions she had long suppressed. Now, she was left with the anticipation of their next meeting, waiting to see if their paths would cross again.

Chapter 2
Needle and Thread

As the hours passed, Mia remained immersed in her work, her heart and mind consumed by thoughts of the dynamic firefighter who had unexpectedly entered her life. In the depths of her logical and reserved soul. Mia allowed herself to entertain thoughts of a possible future together, but anxiety crept in. The idea of being loved and giving love felt messy and unpredictable. Mia cherished the structured, organized life she had built, proud of her successful career. Relationships had always been challenging for her; she feared losing herself and her individuality, and the emotional turmoil from past experiences haunted her. Being single and focusing solely on her job seemed easier and safer.

But Mia couldn't deny the way Jackie made her feel, the undeniable connection that made her heart skip a beat. The warmth of Jackie's smile and the depth in her eyes made Mia feel unexpectedly safe, as if she had always known her. These feelings were confusing to Mia's logical, practical mind. She shrugged the thoughts aside and refocused on her job.

The hands of the clock slowly crept towards 2 a.m., casting a somber ambiance over the now-quiet hospital. Mia, dedicated and tireless, continued her work, but her thoughts kept drifting back to Jackie. The memory of their brief encounter lingered, and she couldn't help but wonder if fate would be kind enough to bring them together once more.

Suddenly, a commotion echoed through the ER, accompanied by the distinct sound of boots treading on the polished floor. Mia turned her head, her heart skipping a beat as she laid eyes on Jackie. The firefighter stood before her, covered in smudges of soot, her uniform marked by the signs of a long and arduous day battling the flames.

Mia couldn't conceal her surprise and concern as she observed Jackie's rumpled appearance. She hurriedly approached, her eyes filled with a mix of curiosity and compassion. "Jackie, what happened? Are you okay?" she asked, her voice betraying her worry.

Jackie, though visibly exhausted, managed to conjure a tired but genuine smile. "I'm back," she said, her voice carrying a hint of relief. "It's been a heck of a night, but I made it."

Mia guided Jackie to a nearby chair, her touch gentle yet purposeful. She couldn't help but notice the fatigue etched across Jackie's face, the flicker of exhaustion in her eyes. As she began to clean Jackie's wounds, her fingers moved with a delicate precision, her touch careful and soothing. However, Mia quickly noticed that the stitches had come undone, and the wound was open and bleeding. She took a deep breath, focusing intently on addressing the reopened injury with swift, professional expertise.

Jackie laid back, her eyelids heavy and drooping, her body worn from the demanding day. Mia could sense the weight Jackie carried, not just physically, but emotionally too. The realization fueled her determination to provide the care Jackie needed.

With a gentle voice, Mia reassured her, "Just relax, Jackie. I'll take care of you. We'll have you patched up in no time."

Jackie managed a weary chuckle, her eyes barely open. "Looks like you're becoming my personal doctor." she murmured, a cheeky remark slipping past her weary lips.

Mia couldn't help but feel a mixture of concern and fondness for Jackie. Her stoicism melted away, replaced by a genuine care and a newfound understanding that blossomed within her. She knew that in this moment, as she cleaned Jackie's wounds and stitched her up once again, there was something more at play, a connection that transcended their roles as doctor and patient.

As Mia worked, the silence of the night enveloped them, their breaths mingling in the hushed room. In that stillness, a sense of vulnerability filled the space between them. Mia understood the weight Jackie carried, the sacrifices she made to keep others safe. And in that understanding, a profound admiration grew.

As the stitches were placed, Jackie's eyes fluttered open, her gaze meeting Mia's. The weariness still lingered, but within the depths of her eyes, gratitude shone through.

"Thank you," Jackie whispered, her voice filled with genuine appreciation. Mia couldn't help but smile, her heart warming at Jackie's words. "It's what I'm here for," she replied softly.

In that quiet moment, as Jackie rested, Mia couldn't deny the burgeoning feelings within her. Their paths had intertwined once again, and Mia realized that this connection, this bond, was far from coincidental. It was a force that would continue to shape their lives, intertwining their destinies in ways they never could have imagined.

As Mia delicately maneuvered the needle, stitching Jackie's wounds, a sudden twinge of pain made Jackie flinch. "Ouch!" she exclaimed, instinctively reaching out and grabbing Mia's arm for support. Their eyes locked, and for a moment, time seemed to stand still.

Caught in the intensity of the moment, Jackie's grip on Mia's arm tightened, their hands connected in a spontaneous act of closeness. Their gazes held a silent conversation.

As Mia felt Jackie's hand firmly grasping her arm, a wave of uncertainty washed over her. Her natural inclination was to pull back, to retreat into the safety of her logical mindset. Confusion clouded her thoughts, and she struggled to make sense of the unexpected feelings that had begun to stir within her.

With a mixture of fear and guarded vulnerability, Mia brushed off Jackie's touch, her voice betraying her unease.

"I..." she stammered, her eyes averting Jackie's gaze. "I'm finished here..." Mia took a step back, creating a physical distance between them, as if it could provide the emotional space she desperately sought. Her professional instincts kicked in, reminding her of the responsibilities she carried as a doctor. She couldn't let her personal desires overshadow the need to ensure Jackie's well-being.

"I've patched you up, and you'll need to stay here for an hour of observation," Mia explained, her tone gentle yet firm. "I'll come back later to check on you."

Jackie, sensing Mia's fear and confusion, simply nodded, understanding the weight of their situation. "Okay," she said softly, her voice tinged with a hint of disappointment.

She could see that Mia was wrestling with her own emotions, trying to reconcile the unexpected connection they shared. As Mia turned to leave, Jackie couldn't help but feel a wave of sadness in her heart.

She watched as Mia walked away, each step carrying a mixture of hesitation and longing. Jackie stood there, her head lowered, feeling a sense of loss for what could have been. In that moment, she silently hoped that Mia would find the courage to embrace the feelings that beckoned her, even if it seemed daunting.

As Mia walked away, the weight of her emotions became too heavy to bear. Overwhelmed by a mix of fear, anger, and confusion, she sought solace in the privacy of a nearby storage room. Closing the door behind her, she leaned against it, her body trembling with pent-up emotions.

Tears welled up in Mia's eyes, and a single teardrop escaped, tracing a path down her cheek. She was frustrated with herself for pushing away the possibility of love, for allowing her own insecurities to cloud her judgment. The surge of emotions within her felt like an unwelcome storm, threatening to dismantle the carefully constructed walls she had built around her heart.

As a doctor, she prided herself on her ability to compartmentalize her emotions, to keep them firmly under control. She had become accustomed to the rigors of her profession, where logic and facts reigned supreme. But now, faced with the overwhelming tide of her own feelings, she felt utterly defenseless.

Her mind, typically sharp and analytical, struggled to understand why these emotions had taken such a hold on her. She questioned her own ability to navigate the intricacies of love, as if her identity as a doctor should somehow shield her from the depths of human emotion. She berated herself for losing control, for allowing her heart to defy the logical boundaries she had so carefully constructed.

Mia found herself at odds with her own nature. How could someone who prided herself on being pragmatic and logical suddenly find herself drowning in a sea of overwhelming emotions? She wondered if this vulnerability was a weakness, a crack in the armor she had so meticulously crafted.

Taking a deep breath, Mia pressed the back of her hand against her cheek, wiping away the tears. Summoning her inner resilience, Mia straightened her posture and let out a resolute sigh. She couldn't let her personal struggles hinder her from fulfilling her responsibilities as a doctor. With renewed determination, she exited the storage room and made her way back to the patients who relied on her care.

***

As time passed, Mia focused on her duties, attending to the medical needs of her patients. She pushed her own feelings aside, burying them deep within, as she went about her work diligently.

But amidst the flurry of activity, a flicker of hope remained within Mia. She couldn't shake off the thoughts of Jackie, the memory of their brief encounter etched into her heart. It was a reminder that love had the power to ignite a fire within, and she couldn't deny the magnetic pull she felt towards Jackie.

As Mia returned to check on Jackie, hoping to find some solace in their connection, her heart sank when she discovered that Jackie had left. The room felt empty, the void of Jackie's absence casting a shadow over Mia's spirit. Regret coursed through her veins, intensifying the longing she felt.

Determined to find answers, Mia approached one of the nurses stationed nearby. Her voice trembled slightly as she inquired, "Excuse me, have you seen Jacqueline Rivera? The firefighter I was attending to earlier? I came to check on her, but she seems to have left."

The nurse glanced up from her paperwork, a hint of sympathy evident in her eyes. "Yes, she left quite abruptly," the nurse responded, her voice tinged with understanding. "She mentioned something about an urgent matter that required her immediate attention."

Mia nodded, her heart sinking further as the reality of Jackie's sudden departure settled in. She felt a mix of emotions—a mixture of disappointment and a longing to reconnect with the woman who had stirred something within her. Questions swirled in her mind, and she couldn't help but wonder if she had missed her chance, if the fragile thread connecting them had been irreparably severed.

As Mia left the room, her steps were heavier than before, weighed down by the unanswered questions and the lingering ache of a missed opportunity.

Chapter 3

Sewing the Edges

Days turned into weeks, and the memory of that fateful encounter continued to haunt Mia. The bustle of the hospital seemed louder, the demands of her work more pronounced, as she tirelessly attended to her duties. Yet, her thoughts often wandered back to Jackie, wondering where she was and if their paths would ever cross again.

Mia found herself caught in a seemingly endless loop of contemplation and what-ifs. She questioned her own actions, grappling with the choice she had made to push Jackie away. The longing for connection clashed with her fear of vulnerability, creating a tug-of-war within her soul.

In the days that followed, Mia couldn't shake Jackie from her mind. She frequently checked the patient log, hoping to see Jackie's name appear among those who had come and gone in the ER. Each time she scanned the list, her heart raced with a mix of anticipation and dread.

Then, one day, to her surprise, she saw Jackie's name on the log. Her pulse quickened, and she immediately asked a nearby nurse, "When did Jacqueline Rivera come in?

The nurse glanced at the log and replied, "She came in yesterday. I think it was for a follow-up on her previous injury."

I wasn't working yesterday, Mia thought to herself. *Did Jackie ask about me? Did she leave a note for me? Maybe it was all in my head, and she was just being nice.*

Mia tried to approach the situation without revealing too much of her emotions. She asked the nurse casually, "I treated her last time. Did she, by any chance, ask for me?"

The nurse, busy with her tasks, glanced up briefly. "I'm not sure," she replied. "I wasn't working on that rotation. You might want to check with someone who was on duty yesterday."

Mia nodded, trying to mask her disappointment. "Okay, thanks," she said, forcing a smile.

As she walked away, her mind raced with thoughts, a knot tightening in her stomach. She replayed their last encounter over and over in her mind, dissecting every word and gesture.

I should have asked more questions. I should have been braver. Why do I always pull back when things get real?

Lost in her introspection, Mia retraced her steps back towards the controlled chaos of the ER where the hum of fluorescent lights and the familiar scent of antiseptic greeted her.

Chapter 4

Tying the Knots

That evening, after a particularly long shift, Mia finally left the hospital, feeling drained from the day's challenges. Thoughts of Jackie had lingered throughout, making the hours feel even longer than usual. As Mia stepped outside, the cool night air offered a welcome relief from the sterile hospital environment.

To her surprise, standing there amidst the faint glow of streetlights was a beautiful woman with lush curly hair, dressed casually in jeans and a leather jacket. It took Mia a moment to register— it was Jackie.

"Jackie?" Mia exclaimed, her voice betraying a mix of surprise and curiosity at the unexpected encounter.

Jackie greeted her with a warm smile. "Hi," she said softly, a hint of shyness in her voice. "I'm sorry I left abruptly the other night. I got called into work, and it's been hectic ever since." She paused, meeting Mia's eyes with sincerity. "I came in yesterday to get my stitches taken off, and I was hoping to find you. The nurse mentioned I might have a chance to catch you tonight, and here we are. I hope that's okay with you."

Mia instinctively reached towards Jackie's forehead, her fingers gently tracing the area where she had placed the stitches. Her touch was soft and careful, a mix of concern and care evident in her actions. "How's your head feeling?" she asked, her voice laced with genuine worry.

Jackie closed her eyes momentarily, savoring the warmth of Mia's touch. "It's much better, thanks to you," she replied softly.

how close they were, Mia quickly withdrew her hand, her cheeks flushing slightly. "It healed nicely," she said, her tone more professional now, though her eyes still held a trace of warmth.

Jackie looked at Mia, her eyes reflecting a mix of sincerity and a touch of nervous excitement. "I wanted to see you again, to thank you for helping me," she confessed, her smile widening as she gathered her courage. She took a deep breath and continued, "And, I was wondering if you'd like to go out for dinner sometime?"

There was a subtle tremor in her voice, a vulnerability peeking through her usual confidence. She leaned slightly forward, her gaze earnestly fixed on Mia's, willing her words to convey just how much she wanted this moment to be right.

Mia stood there, momentarily speechless. Her logical mind wrestled with the rush of emotions swirling inside her. As she looked into Jackie's eyes, the walls around her heart began to soften. The connection they had shared, however brief, had left a mark on both of them. A smile tugged at the corners of Mia's lips, matching the radiance of Jackie's. She found herself unable to resist the magnetic pull between them, the undeniable chemistry that had sparked from their first encounter.

Mia nodded, her voice filled with a mixture of vulnerability and reserved excitement. "I would love that," she replied, her words carrying a weight of sincerity. "I'm actually free now for dinner if you are too," she added with a soft smile.

Jackie smiled warmly. "Do you like Mexican food? I know a great little place close by," she asked.

Mia's face softened into a smile. "I love Mexican," she said calmly. "Lead the way."

Chapter 5

Holding in Place

The Mexican restaurant buzzed with a lively atmosphere as Jackie and Mia settled into a cozy corner booth, away from the bustling crowd. Mariachi music played in the background, adding to the relaxed vibe of the evening. They browsed the menu, occasionally exchanging smiles and small talk.

"I love this place," Jackie said, her eyes twinkling with enthusiasm. "It's my favorite spot in town."

Mia nodded in agreement, her expression lighting up. "I've never been here before ," she replied warmly.

As they placed their orders for food and drinks, the conversation flowed effortlessly.

They shared stories about work, their interests outside of their professions, and their favorite travel destinations. The initial nervousness melted away, replaced by a comfortable connection that seemed to grow with each passing moment.

Both relaxed now, Mia leaned forward slightly, her curiosity sparked. "So, what was that other thing you were going to tell me about? Venus or something in astrology?" Despite her skepticism, Mia's tone carried a hint of genuine interest, showing that their previous conversation had left an impression on her and intrigued her enough to want to learn more.

Jackie smiled warmly, her eyes lighting up with enthusiasm. "Ah, so you're ready for lesson 2 then," she teased gently. Leaning in a bit closer, she began to explain, "Venus is the planet of love in astrology. It shows how you give and receive love, what brings you joy, and how you approach relationships."

She continued, her voice taking on a thoughtful tone, "I have Venus in Scorpio, which is a water sign known for its intensity and depth."

Mia glanced at Jackie with a curious expression, though the word "intense" made her uneasy. She didn't know exactly what Jackie meant by that and felt wary of emotionally intense people. "So, you're... intense in relationships?" she asked, trying to mask her discomfort.

Jackie paused, her gaze piercing yet soft as she looked into Mia's eyes. "When I love, I love deeply. I give it my all. I'm all in."

Mia looked at her, feeling uneasy. She didn't say anything for a moment, processing Jackie's words. Jackie noticed her hesitation and gently asked, "What about you? What are you like in relationships?"

Mia felt a wave of awkwardness wash over her. She didn't know how to respond, feeling vulnerable discussing such personal matters. She stuttered slightly, "I... I don't know.

Confused, I guess," she said with an awkward laugh.

This moment revealed a side of Mia she rarely showed. She didn't like talking about her emotions, preferring to keep her vulnerabilities hidden. Jackie, noticing Mia's discomfort, gently reached across the table and took her hand. "Hey... it's okay. We don't have to talk about this," she said softly, letting the conversation drift back to lighter topics to help Mia feel at ease again.

Mia was touched by the gesture and looked into Jackie's eyes, getting lost in their depth. She could feel her heart beating faster, but she instinctively pulled her hand away and broke the gaze. Her emotional insecurities were triggered. Her body language changed; she sat more rigidly, her shoulders tense. Her gaze darted around the restaurant, searching for an escape route, while her hands fidgeted nervously with the napkin in her lap. Insecurity and fear clawed at the edges of her mind, urging her to retreat and protect herself once again. The fragile connection they were building seemed to hang in the balance, and Mia struggled to find her footing amidst the storm of her emotions.

Jackie felt the energy shift, just like that night in the ER. The lively, relaxed atmosphere they had shared only moments before seemed to evaporate, replaced by a palpable tension. She watched as Mia's body language became more guarded, her shoulders tensing and her eyes darting around the room.

Mia's fingers fidgeted nervously with the napkin in her lap, a clear sign of her growing unease. Jackie could sense the insecurity and fear that seemed to be consuming Mia, urging her to retreat and put up her defenses once more.

Mia hesitated, a flicker of unease crossing her features as she looked at Jackie. "I had a really good time," she began slowly, "But I think I need to go." Her movements became abrupt as she started to gather her things, a sense of urgency in her actions that betrayed her unease.

Jackie watched Mia gather her things, taken aback by how quickly the mood had shifted. With a concerned expression, she spoke softly, "Mia, is everything okay?" Her voice carried a hint of worry, sensing Mia's unease and wanting to understand what had changed so suddenly.

Mia nodded, her voice tinged with unease. "Everything's fine, I just need to leave," she said quietly, offering no further explanation.

Jackie stood up, a concerned look on her face. "Let me at least walk you back to your car," she insisted gently.

"It's really not necessary," Mia insisted, her tone firm yet tinged with reluctance.

Chapter 6

Healing

Mia left the restaurant in a whirlwind of emotions, embarrassment, upset, and a hint of anger directed inward. She felt frustrated with herself for not being able to control her feelings, for not understanding what she was experiencing. This uncertainty left her unsettled, unable to make sense of her own emotions.

For years, she had navigated through medical school and residency by shutting down her emotions, focusing solely on the tasks at hand. It was her coping mechanism, her way of pushing through challenges. Now, faced with unfamiliar feelings and vulnerability, she instinctively retreated to this familiar strategy.

Keep moving forward, keep emotions at bay, that had been her mantra for so long.

As Mia hurried across the street, trying to put distance between herself and the restaurant, she could hear faint calls of her name behind her. Heart pounding, she quickened her pace, hoping to escape the turmoil inside her.

Cutting through a nearby park, Mia sought solace in the quietude of the night. The soft rustling of leaves and distant city sounds provided a stark contrast to the chaos in her mind. Just as she began to feel a semblance of calm, footsteps approached from behind.

Jackie hurried to catch up with Mia, her footsteps echoing softly on the pavement. As she reached Mia, she gently reached out and took her hand, stopping Mia in her tracks. "Mia, wait... just wait a sec," Jackie said, her voice calm yet determined.

Mia tried to avoid Jackie's gaze, her stance subtly standoffish. She felt the strength of Jackie's presence, a mix of concern and sincerity that made it difficult to maintain her guarded facade. Despite her attempt to remain distant, Mia couldn't help but feel a flicker of vulnerability in Jackie's touch and voice.

"Hey, Mia, what's wrong? Talk to me. Is it something I said? I apologize if I made you feel uncomfortable," Jackie said, her voice filled with concern.

Mia, unable to look her in the eyes, replied, "No, it's not that. I just..."

Jackie continued to look at her, waiting. "It's just... I don't know if I can do this, okay."

"Do what?" Jackie asked softly.

"This thing that's happening between us. I don't know what this is or what it means, and it's happening so quickly," Mia admitted, her voice trembling.

Jackie looked at Mia with a mix of confusion and concern as they stood under the soft moonlight. Mia ran a hand through her hair, feeling the weight of her own words. "We just met," she began, her voice wavering slightly. "We don't know each other, and I just... I can't feel like this. This isn't me. I don't know how to do this..."

Jackie looked at Mia and gently placed her hand on her shoulder. "I don't know how to do this either. I've never felt this way before," she admitted softly. Pausing for a moment, she met Mia's eyes with sincerity. "I feel a deep connection with you, Mia. It's indescribable. Love isn't something you do; it's something you are, and I want to share my love with you."

Mia stood there, her eyes welling up with tears. "But I'm not like you, Jackie. I'm not brave and adventurous like you. I don't know if I can..."

Before she could finish, Jackie gently pulled her closer and whispered, "Shhh." She moved in slowly, and Mia felt Jackie's soft lips pressing against her own. The kiss was gentle and tender, sending a warm sensation through Mia's body. She felt herself melting into the kiss as their lips moved effortlessly together.

Mia's logical mind faded away, replaced by pure, raw emotion. She could feel her heart opening and electric sensations pulsating through her body. She gave in to the feeling, throwing her arms around Jackie and deepening the kiss. As their lips danced to the rhythm of their heartbeat, Mia felt as if she was breathing one breath with Jackie, as if they were merged into one. Jackie ran her hands through Mia's hair, and Mia felt her head tingle. They kissed underneath the moonlight, and it felt like eternity.

In that moment, all fears and doubts were washed away by the depth of their connection. They pulled back slightly, their foreheads touching, breathing in unison. Mia looked into Jackie's eyes and saw the reflection of her own emotions, vulnerability, hope, and an undeniable bond.

Jackie smiled softly, her hand gently caressing Mia's cheek. "You stitched me up, Doctor Mia Carella. Now let me stitch that little heart of yours. I promise to be gentle."

Mia laughed, a sound full of relief and newfound joy. She threw her arms around Jackie and kissed her. Under the moonlight, they shared a tender moment, their hearts beating in unison. As they embraced, time seemed to stop. The world around them faded away, leaving only the warmth of their connection. In that perfect moment, they both felt a profound sense of belonging and love. It was as if they had known each other forever, and the future stretched out before them, full of promise and possibilities. Together, they began a new chapter, one filled with hope, understanding, and a love that would heal and grow, one stitch at a time.

The End